THE FISH SKIN

For Luke

The author is indebted to the Cree people of Norway House and Cross Lake. The legends of Wîsahkecàhk were told to the author by the elders of these communities. The story in this book is a retelling of one of these legends. Many authorities were consulted to put the story in the correct setting. Special thanks to Dr. Katherine Pettipas, Curator of Native Ethnology, Manitoba Museum of Man and Nature; Dr. John Nichols, Professor of Native Studies, University of Manitoba; Ida Bear, Research and Planning, Manitoba Association for Native Languages Inc.; Philip Paynter, Aboriginal Liaison Officer, Winnipeg School Division No. 1; Leo Pettipas, Consultant on Native Heritage Issues; and Calvin Pompana, Aboriginal Administrator, Winnipeg, Manitoba.

Text © 1993 by Jamie Oliviero.
Illustrations © 1993 by Brent Morrisseau. All rights reserved.
Printed in Hong Kong. For more information address Hyperion Books for Children, 114 Fifth Avenue, New York, New York 10011.

FIRST EDITION

1 3 5 7 9 10 8 6 4 2

Library of Congress Catalog Card Number: 92-85509
ISBN: 1-56282-401-5/1-56282-402-3 (lib. bdg.)

This book is set in 16-point Palatino.
The illustrations are prepared in gouache art medium.
Designed by A. O. Osen

Printed in Hong Kong

THE FISH SKIN

JAMIE OLIVIERO

ILLUSTRATED BY
BRENT MORRISSEAU

Hyperion Books for Children
New York

Long ago in the Land of the North Wind, as Grandfather Sun moved in splendor across the sky, he chanced to look down into a large, clear lake. Surprised by his reflection in the still water, he was distracted for a moment from his course across the heavens. As he paused, his warmth lingered over the people who were camped beside the lake, and they were pleased. They were tired of Cloud's shade and rain, and they asked Cloud to stay away.

Grandfather Sun shone brighter and brighter over the people's camp. Without Cloud's protection, the days became hotter and hotter, and soon the land was parched and dry.

Finally it was so hot that Beaver did not have the strength to lift his tail to slap the water. Wolf's throat was so dry that when she tried to howl, nothing came out but a dusty cough.

Turtle's shell, which had been as smooth as stone, was now covered with lines and cracks. Even people's shadows seemed to melt on the ground behind them. The nights hardly cooled the land, and the daily presence of Grandfather Sun made the people miserable.

In the camp, a young boy lived with his grandmother.
As the days grew steadily warmer, Grandmother
became weaker. The boy tried to care for her but soon
realized that unless the rains came, Grandmother—
and others—would die.

Who will help us? the boy thought. Then he remembered Grandmother's stories about the forest on the other side of the camp and the Great Spirit who lived there. Grandmother said his name was Wìsahkecàhk (wes-a-KEH-jak) and that he was the maker and shaper of many things. The boy decided that he must visit Wìsahkecàhk and ask him to make it rain.

That night, when the air had cooled slightly, the boy set out alone. He had never been in the forest at night by himself, and every sound and every shadow frightened him.

Finally he was too tired and frightened to go any farther. He sat down beside an old tree, hugged his knees to his chest, and hid his head so he wouldn't see the moving shapes of the night. After a while he fell asleep.

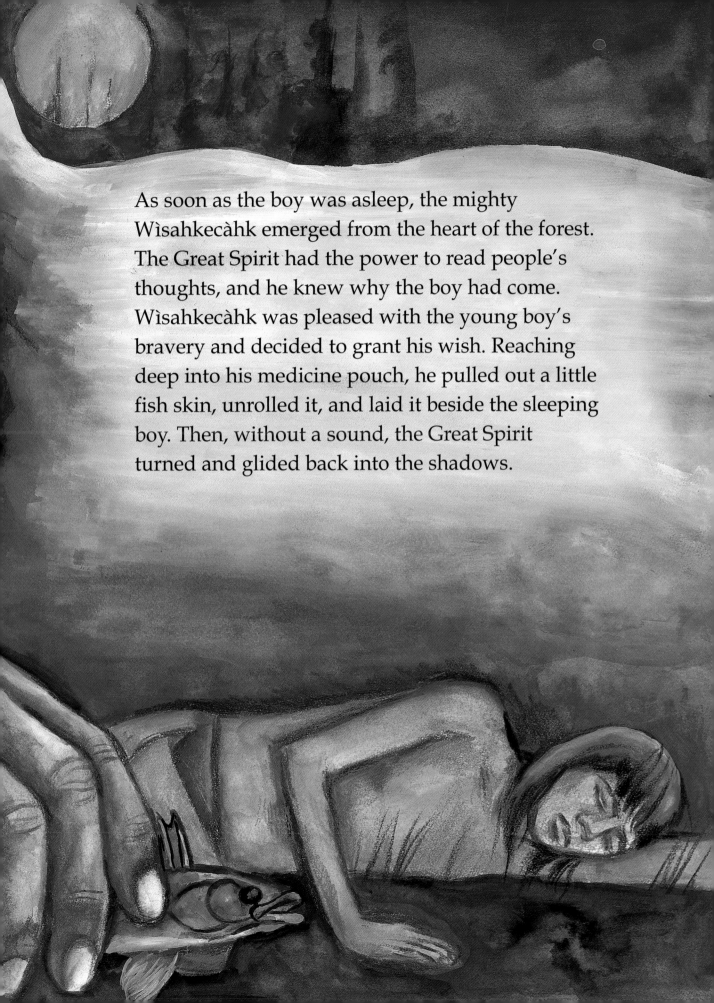

As soon as the boy was asleep, the mighty
Wìsahkecàhk emerged from the heart of the forest.
The Great Spirit had the power to read people's
thoughts, and he knew why the boy had come.
Wìsahkecàhk was pleased with the young boy's
bravery and decided to grant his wish. Reaching
deep into his medicine pouch, he pulled out a little
fish skin, unrolled it, and laid it beside the sleeping
boy. Then, without a sound, the Great Spirit
turned and glided back into the shadows.

At dawn the boy awoke. He held up the strange fish skin and tried to put it on. The fish skin stretched and stretched until the boy was able to slide it up his body and pull it over his head. It fit him perfectly.

Now the boy not only looked like a fish but also had the powers of one. He flopped down to the lake and dived in. The water was cool and refreshing. Deeper and deeper he swam. Then he began to drink. He drank so much that he swelled up to an enormous size and looked quite fierce.

Then he swam to the surface, stuck his head out of the water, and called to Cloud.

"The people need rain," he said.

"They have learned that Nature's cycle is good. Now they value Cloud's refreshing shade and rain as well as Grandfather Sun's gift of light and warmth."

The boy in the fish skin called again, and soon Cloud spread over the lake.

Then the boy in the fish skin opened his fishy lips and blew out all the water that he had drunk. He blew hard and high so that the water bounced off Cloud and fell back down as rain.

All the creatures and all the people came running out from where they were hiding under the shade trees to stand in the cool water.

Beaver was so happy that he slapped his tail in every puddle he could find. Wolf let the water slide down her throat and howled for joy.

The boy wriggled out of the fish skin, rolled it up, and carried it home to Grandmother. He helped her out into the rain, and soon her strength returned.

When the boy told Grandmother about the fish skin, she knew that it was a gift from Wìsahkecàhk. "From now on," she said, "you will be called Okwàpayikêw (oh-kwaw-PAY-eh-kew, which means 'water hauler')." The boy was very pleased. Then Grandmother took the fish skin and put it in a safe place in case they should ever need it again.

All this time Turtle was crawling out from under the trees, but he moved so slowly that by the time he reached the clearing the rain had stopped. He did not enjoy its restoring powers. That is why, to this day, Turtle still has cracks and lines on his shell.

The Cree have a 3,500-year-old history
in the Land of the North Wind —
the dense, subarctic boreal forest of
northern Manitoba, Ontario, and
Quebec in Canada.
The idea of their universe is the circle,
which represents the unity and
harmony of all things. Everything
in Nature has an equal place
within the circle, including rivers,
rocks, earth, sky, plants, animals,
and humans.
All of these have spirit and life.
In order to preserve the circle,
every being must live in harmony
with every other being
and perform its prescribed function.
When this does not happen,
the harmony is broken,
and some sort of supernatural
intervention
is required to set it right.